Ten Little Monkeys jumping on the bed

illustrated by
Tina Freeman

Child's Play (International) Ltd
Ashworth Rd, Bridgemead, Swindon, SN5 7YD UK
Swindon Auburn ME Sydney

Printed in Heshan, China
ISBN 978-0-85953-888-6 HH120313NBH05138886
15 17 19 20 18 16 14
www.childs-play.com

Ten little monkeys
jumping on the bed,

One fell off
and bumped his head.

Mother called the doctor,

And the doctor said,
"No more monkeys
jumping on the bed!"

Nine little monkeys
jumping on the bed,

One fell off
and bumped her head.

Mother called the doctor,

And the doctor said,

"No more monkeys
jumping on the bed!"

Eight little monkeys
jumping on the bed,

One fell off
and bumped his head.

Mother called the doctor,

And the doctor said,
"No more monkeys
jumping on the bed!"

Seven little monkeys
jumping
on the bed,

One fell off
and bumped his head.

Mother called the doctor,

And the doctor said,
"No more monkeys
jumping on the bed!"

Six little monkeys
jumping on the bed,

One fell off
and bumped his head.

Mother called the doctor,

And the doctor said,
"No more monkeys
jumping on the bed!"

Five little monkeys
jumping on the bed,
One fell off
and bumped her head.

Mother called
the doctor,

And the doctor said,
"No more monkeys
jumping on the bed!"

Four little monkeys
jumping on the bed,
One fell off
and bumped her head.

Mother called
the doctor,

And the doctor said,
"No more monkeys
jumping on the bed!"

Three little monkeys
jumping on the bed,
One fell off
and bumped his head.

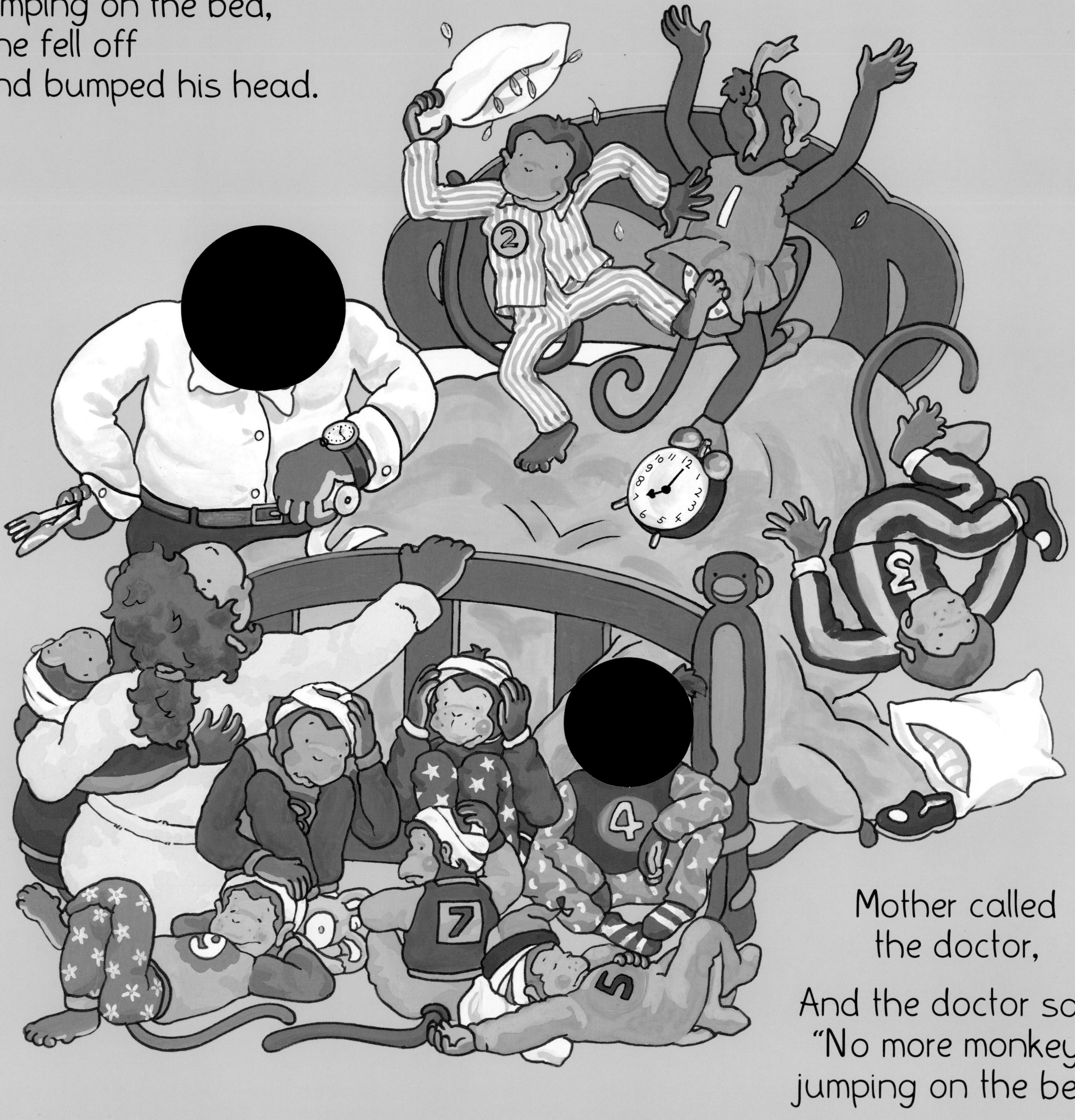

Mother called
the doctor,

And the doctor said,
"No more monkeys
jumping on the bed!"

Two little monkeys
jumping on the bed,
One fell off
and bumped his head.

Mother called
the doctor,

And the doctor said,
"No more monkeys
jumping on the bed!"

One little monkey
jumping on the bed,
She fell off
and bumped her head.

Mother called
the doctor,

And the doctor said,

"NO MORE MONKEYS
JUMPING ON THE BED!"